That's when they trapped us, those star-children. After that moment, we couldn't say no to them; we could only offer them the shelter of our home, and let them do whatever on earth they wanted.

Three strange, carefully wrapped infants appear on a Bethlehem rubbish heap—local girl Leah doesn't like their looks, but her little sister Shoshana insists on bringing them home.

That night, in a stable across town, a woman goes into labour. Hers is a very special baby, announced by angels, its birthplace marked by a star. But her husband Yoseph looks into baby Emmanuel's eyes and wonders, is this really the Son of the Lord, or just of a simple carpenter?

And then the visitors arrive.

Margo Lanagan's Christmas novelette is a dance along the border between faith and fantasy. Which side will you fall down on?

We Three Kids

This first edition of *We Three Kids*
is limited to 500 copies
of which this copy is

WE THREE KIDS

MARGO LANAGAN

2013

WE THREE KIDS

FIRST EDITION

ISBN
978-1-848637-03-0

Design and layout by Michael Smith

Printed and bound in England by T.J. International

PS Publishing Ltd
Grosvenor House
1 New Road
Hornsea, HU18 1PG
England

editor@pspublishing.co.uk | www.pspublishing.co.uk

Leah

It all started yesterday, late in the afternoon. Only so recently! Mother was building up the fire to cook our evening meal, Father chatting in his shoutiest voice with a customer in the workshop. I'd brought the wood from the market, and now I leaned in the house doorway. The sky was turning orange over the housetops opposite.

Shoshana skidded to a stop in the laneway there, and stood panting. "Leah, come."

I should have told her to leave me in peace. "Come where?" I said. "For what?"

"Just . . . " She beckoned with one hand, put a finger to her lips with the other.

She's generally a good girl, little Shoshie. She does what she's told and doesn't make mischief. So I followed her; we sped along the laneways out of town, straight across the bare ground all the kids use for games and races.

"I know where you're taking me," I said. "Father told us not to play in the dump, didn't he?"

"I wasn't playing," she said over her shoulder. "I only walked by and heard them. And I thought, *That's not kittens.*"

"Oh, what have you gone and found, Shosh?"

"Hey!" And there was Matti, running after us. He must have seen us from the back of Abiud's place where he'd gone to play. "Where are you two off to?"

"Oh, good," said Shoshie. "You can help carry them." She ran on, with her arm up as if holding the end of a string. And we followed as if pulled along by that string, as if we had no wills of our own.

"She's found something at the dump," I said. "Some live thing."

Matti's face lit up, of course. I should've told him to go home. I should've gone myself.

Along the road we hurried after Shosh, and all the smells were stronger in the cooling air: the dust and stones underfoot and the fresh dung there from someone's donkey, and the shitty smell of somebody's freshly fertilized field nearby and the foul sweetness of something rotting in the dump ahead. *You are not rubbish pickers,* our father once told us. *You are the sandal-man's children. You've no call to be digging about in that filth, and coming home stinking of poverty and death.*

But it's full of useful stuff, Matti had said. *Like . . . I don't know. Some of those oil jars are hardly even chipped!*

It's full of pestilence, is what it's full of. We have jars of our own—we've no need of other people's leavings.

Of course, as Father probably knew, we didn't go to the dump for useful things; we went there to scare ourselves and make ourselves sick, with the way dead rats and dogs and the occasional poor person melted down to gluey dark skin and bones, the way carrion birds rearranged themselves and greedily watched us, hoping for first peck of our bright juicy eyeballs. It was interesting to find a shard of something and try to work out what it might have been, or to lift up some nearly perfect lamp or pot and smash it down among the other bits and bones: it was fun to poke at the corpse of something with a stick and then wave that stick at your brother and make him shout. We went there when we were angry or bored; the horrible things we found there made us grateful for our home again, how clean it was, and sweet-smelling.

Shoshie was at the mounds now, climbing in among them. "Oh no-no-no," I said. "Don't let her."

"What can it be?" Matti drew ahead of me.

He turned back for a moment, wide-eyed, as they cried out, all three at once and just the single cry. We came right up to the edge of the dump, and they called again. Shosh was right, it wasn't kittens.

"Some kind of bird?" said Matti. "Something has made a nest, and these have hatched in it?"

"That's never a hatchling anything," I said. "That's something *old*. That's nearly *words*." And I still think that's true. Though they seemed so helpless, right from the beginning, I reckon, they knew what they were doing, what they could get away with.

Shoshie was not far in and there was nothing particularly revolting along the way, although it all smelled bad, and one pile sank under our sandals, making us hurry more than I wanted to. Shoshie was bent over, talking at something. "— with my brother and sister, too!" she finished in a sing-song voice, and then she stood aside, wobbled, steadied herself and turned to us, all eager.

"It's *babies*!" said Matti.

And I thought, *Really? Those stiff little things?* Then I had to concentrate on my footing over a pile of dry old sheep and goats' bones, and then I was on firmer stuff and looking straight down into their three faces.

"Eugh," said Matti quietly at my shoulder.

"There's something wrong with those," I said. Shoshie's face fell, but I couldn't bring myself to be kinder. "Whoever they belong to doesn't want them. That's why they've been put here. "

"They weren't *put*," she said. "They're star-children. They just *came*."

The back of my neck felt as if a spider were tiptoeing across it. "What a thing to say! Who told you that?"

"*They* did," she said. "You only have to look at them—"

"What do you mean, *star*-children?" I hoped my scorn would shock some sense into her. "There's no such thing! These babies are no shinier than any others. "

"I don't know." She checked them as if they might have suddenly started to glow. "I don't know what it means. It's just what they are."

I took a breath, but no words came to me, and I only shook my head.

"They're very neatly wrapped." Matti shifted position next to me and something underneath us creaked and snapped. "They're *perfectly* wrapped. That would have taken ages, so neat and criss-cross like that."

"See?" I said. "Whoever put them here must have meant for them to die. Must have meant to never unwrap them again."

They had shiny dark eyes, all three of them, and funny-shaped faces, wide in the cheekbones and pointy in the chin. And old, yes. Maybe it was from being left out starving under the sky. If they'd been actually dead they wouldn't have worried me so much, but the shriveled faces *and* those bright eyes looking up? It looked wrong, and it made me *feel* wrong.

But they obviously didn't make Shoshie feel wrong. Her chin poked out, and I could tell my scorn hadn't worked. I softened my voice and tried to sound more reasonable. "Three babies—maybe that's just too many mouths for their family to feed. Come on, Shoshie, they're none of our business." And I turned away, grabbing Matti's sleeve to turn him too.

"But don't you think—" he said.

"If we each take one!" said Shoshie. "They're *quite* clean, look!"

"Home, Shosh." I tossed the words over my shoulder, trying to sound cross and sensible. "They'll wonder where we are. And don't pick up any smells on the way back."

"I'll carry them *myself*, then!" she said. "It's all right, I can manage. They're only small—"

"Shoshie, no!" I swung back. "Put it down. Don't even touch them!" Too late. She bent for the next one, staggering with the weight of the first. "Shosh, just *leave* them! They're safe on the ground! At least they can't fall anywhere!"

Carrying the two, she lurched across the rubbish, her face red. "I'll come back for that other one." She stopped and hoisted a baby higher with her knee.

"Shoshie!"

"I'll bring the other," said Matti, and was suddenly gone from my side. He does that sometimes, just calmly takes over, sounding all calm and grown-up, making *me* sound all bossy and pretend-y.

I don't know how else to be, though. "Matti, this is stupid! We can't bring home three babies!"

But he had the baby in his arms, his face quite serious. "I know," he said. "But Mother will know what to do. Where we should take them. They don't have to stay with *us*."

Shoshie made to march right past me. Both babies were slipping down her front, one worse than the other, but she didn't meet my eye, and her mouth was clamped closed; she was determined not to ask for help.

"Here, you're dropping him." I took hold of the lower baby.

"Will you bring him?" She kept gripping. "You can't have him if you're just going to put him back."

"Are you *serious*?" I said to Matti.

He shrugged and made a face around the baby-cylinder he held. "We can't just leave babies lying *crying*—"

"They're *not* crying," I said. "They're—"

"Of *course* they're not," Shoshie snapped. "They're rescued now; they don't *need* to make a noise."

"Don't be silly. Babies aren't sensible like that." The baby was as hard and straight against me as a wooden post. "You're just inventing stuff, to make us do what you want."

Shoshie didn't bother answering; she was too busy slipping and sliding down the clinking bone-heap. Her baby stared out over her shoulder with no expression on its face; the shaking didn't trouble it.

Matti passed me, rocking his head from side to side as if he was just doing what Shoshie wanted for the sake of peace. So

I sort of had to follow them, then. I couldn't just stand there in the rubbish whining after them.

I thought someone would stop us when we got in among the houses, and ask us where these strange babies came from; I *hoped* someone would, so we could hand the things over and walk away from them. But we didn't meet *anyone* we knew, not the whole way home. I was too busy, at the time, trying to think up some other way to get rid of them, but now I wonder, where *was* everyone? Where were the kids running around in the lanes, and the grown-ups leaning in doorways talking to each other? Did those babies *organize* for the streets to be empty? Can star-children do that?

We filed into our own house and lined up where Mother could see us. Well, you can imagine. At first she thought we'd stolen them, and she could hardly speak, she was so scared and angry. "No, they were at the *dump*," I said. "Shoshie heard them crying and went to find them." Then Shoshie piped up with her star-children nonsense. Mother looked bewildered, so I pounced on Shosh again. "You keep *saying* that—but what does it mean? What *is* a star-child?"

Father came to the workshop doorway. He went so exactly through what Mother had just gone through that I might have thought it was funny if I hadn't had this hard-wrapped *thing* clutched to me and two other creepy shrivel-faces in the room. But my arms were aching, and the baby seemed to be growing heavier by the moment. While they exclaimed back and forth, I sank to my knees and laid my bundle on the floor. I could have sworn it hadn't been as big as that at the dump; it stared back at me, daring me to remember the size, try to picture Shoshie standing beside it in the rubbish.

"How do you undo these things?" Matti lowered his baby to the floor beside mine. He tipped it to one side to examine the bindings up its back. I pointed on mine to where the cloth was tucked in under the chin, and he found the same place on his and pulled it free and began unwinding.

"Why are you doing that?" I said. "It's not fussing."

"Just to see if there *is* something wrong with it. Some hidden thing. Some reason they threw it away."

Mother, and Father close beside her, had stopped trying to get Shoshie to talk sense. Father's hands were on his hips, and Mother's went to her mouth as Matti unwound and unwound. The bundle grew less log-like; arms became clearer within the cloth, pressed tight to the body. It was a long, thin baby, and its head was much too big. Its legs were flattened out straight and its feet had a little piece of wood underneath them, a tiny floor to stand on.

Finally all the cloth was off, and it lay there, a little boy, uncurled, unbabylike, who looked up at Matti, as if thinking, *Why did you bother doing all that work?* And then, between one of my glances and the next, he grew again. He didn't swell up fatter; he was simply a little bit bigger all over than before. And my baby next to him was bigger again too, and its bundle was bigger to hold it. I didn't imagine this—I could tell I didn't, because Mother and Father and Matti all made surprised noises, and Shoshie swayed because *her* baby was suddenly heavier too. Mother and Father stepped forward and caught hold of it so as she wouldn't drop it—and there we were, each touching one of the things. Looking back, I'm thinking that that's when they trapped us, those star-children. After that moment, we couldn't say no to them; we could only offer them the shelter of our home, and let them do whatever on earth they wanted.

Yoseph

In the middle of the night, she reaches through the straw and shakes me. And though my sleep is so black, so soft, so well deserved, I allow it to shred and the stable's smells and the memories to crowd in, of our days' travelling and our evening's searching and negotiating for this straw and this shelter.

"It's coming," she hisses at my ear. "The pains keep coming."

A cry—small yet, and woeful—is forced out of her. I lift my head from the blanket and push myself out of the crackling straw.

She's a darker darkness, breathing hard. "Light the lamp."

"She didn't give us much oil, that woman, remember. She didn't want her stable going up in flames, she said—"

"Light it!" She sounds weepy.

I put my hand on her arm. "We'll wait," I say. "This could go on for hours yet. For *days.*"

She sways horrified in the straw. "Should you fetch that innkeeper's wife?" she says.

"Now, what would we need her for?" I hear my mother's vague, tranquil tone in my own voice. "Haven't we talked about this? I've seen more babies born, dead and alive and monstrous too, than any innkeeper's wife has." Once upon a time Mother midwifed for everyone here in Bethlehem, and she dragged Paz and me about with her. I know what to do better than most husbands, better even than some wives. "Besides, that wife, she was so unpleasant, Mariam. You don't want her sneering face to be the first the boy sees." I don't know what he'll be like, this Son of the Lord, but common sense tells me to make things nice for his arrival.

And if this child is going to be what the angels say he is, the three of us need to be a strong little family, sufficient unto ourselves in as many ways as we can be. Or at least, that's what I tell myself. There's also a large part of me that just wants it to be me, Mariam and the baby, for the angels to have been only dreams and the baby to be only a baby, unheralded and ordinary, a son to help me in my workshop, and to inherit it when I'm gone. A man needs no more than that.

"Another one's coming!"

"Kiss the fear goodbye, Mariam," I say. "Breathe as you'd breathe at any midnight, in and out. Keep your throat open, calm your heart."

She whimpers, shifts. The straw hisses around her, just as irritable as she. "Women *die* of this."

I chuckle. "Nobody dies of these first few pangs, don't you worry. And as for later, you're my Mariam, young and strong and sensible. You'll be done by morning." *You have to say that to them,* says Mother; *they don't believe you, but it helps make it true, gives them something to aim for.* "And the Son of the Lord in your arms."

That quietens her. What is that going to mean? we wonder. What's it going to be like?

And so, after all our journeying, we begin along the road of my wife's labour. It's the same as every other labour, one hill after another to crest, one valley after another to gather strength in—but it's different too, of course, because she's mine. It's different from being a bored boy in a house full of waiting women, forbidden from teasing Paz while they organize this baby out. It's different because it's Mariam, my wife, whom I know as I never knew any of those mothers I saw in my youth, who all seemed so old, and so ugly in their pain. It's different because I'm older myself now, and I know that they weren't, as I thought, just greedy for attention, just making noise to hurt my ears. "Rest now," I say as Mariam's each pain eases. "Freshen yourself for the next one." And she puts her head on my shoulder and sinks away for a moment's sleep. My whole life has been preparing me for this night.

Leah

Matti bound his baby back up as well as he could, and Mother unwrapped the other two. "Maybe one of them is monstrous enough to condemn all three. You never know how people think, especially new mothers and fathers." One baby was a girl and the last another boy. She checked that their behinds were clean and swaddled them up again, slowly and carefully, keeping to the same criss-cross pattern.

We washed our hands and prayed and ate. We tried to persuade the babies to eat, or to sup on some milk, but their little withered tongues pushed all food and drink straight back out of their mouths.

"To sleep, then," said Mother. "These gleamy eyes look as if they'll never close, but we must have our rest."

The babies didn't need a bed; their beds were all wrapped around them, and so tightly that they didn't have a chance of wriggling free. And nobody wanted them in the sleeping room with us, even though they were perfectly quiet—their quietness was one of the wrongest things about them. So we just laid them along the wall where no one would trip on them in the dark, and took ourselves to our beds.

They did not squeak all night. "I can't even hear them breathing," Mother whispered to Father, and we all lay still to listen. "Can you remember whether they breathed, whether their chests rose and fell?"

"Of course they breathed," Father blustered quietly. "Weak with starvation, that's their problem."

"If they survive the night," said Mother, "we must ask old mother Chava's opinion tomorrow, whether we should force any form of food on them at all."

I didn't want to go to sleep with those babies in the house. I was afraid they would shuck off their wrappings in the night, get up, come to the door and *look* at us while we slept. I didn't know what they might do beyond that; the looking was frightening enough, those unblinking eyes, those wide bony faces, and the darkness all around.

Sleep carried me off anyway. But I'd spent so long looking at the babies that I dreamed about them all night, about their silence and stiffness. I dreamed that we shook them to make them speak, that we took them out of their bundles and picked up their limpness, their bony heads dangling and disapproving of us upside down. I dreamed that they broke apart in our hands, but the pieces stayed alive, the eyes still watching, the little old hands clasping things. I woke up shuddering, and reached out to touch Matti, warm and solid beside me. He breathed just the way a real person should breathe in sleep, easily, openly, trusting that all was well outside his eyelids.

In the morning we kids lay pretending to sleep on, waiting for someone else to be the first to rise. Finally a dream threw Father out of sleep, and he gasped and snuffled. "How late it is!" He sat up, and we all looked back at him. "Why didn't you wake me? We have all those orders from yesterday, and there'll be more customers today!" He scrambled up, and we threw back our blankets.

But he stopped at the door. "The Lord strike me!"

"What, Father?" said Matti. "Are they gone?" I sprang right to my feet at the joyful possibility.

"No," said Father. "They're twice as much here as they were yesterday."

The babies lay along the wall, but not lined up the way we'd left them. They'd grown again in the night, and in their growing had pushed up against each other, pushed each other aside. One, the girl, lay on her side with her head by her brother's knees. The other brother was wedged face to the wall; Mother went and lifted him free. "There, is that better?" she said, but he seemed just as discontented as the others.

"Oh, look what's come underneath him." She brought out a fourth baby, much smaller than the others, its binding-cloths hardly wider than tie-tapes such as hold up thin drawers or shirt necks.

She waved it, and I gasped, for I'd thought it alive. "A dolly!" she said. "A dolly of themselves. I can't think where it's slipped out from."

She tossed it to Father and he bent over it. How enormous he looked, with his morning-creased face, his wild hair and his beard like thick smoke! The doll-baby's face, by contrast, was all delicate and composed, the eyes carved shut. I wouldn't like to be it, and wake, and find that giant above me.

"How did they get so much bigger?" Mother crouched by the wall and took the boy-baby into her lap, looked it up and down, weighed it in her arms. "Without so much as eating a crumb or taking a sip?" She shook her head over the great parcel of him. "From the stars, you say, Shoshie?"

Shoshie moved her shoulders—was she embarrassed, or could she just not be bothered keeping on with that story? Father passed her the dolly and she held it gingerly, looked at it all over, handed it quickly on to Matti.

"How did they tell you they were star-children?" said Mother. "With their actual mouths?"

Shoshie raised her face and met Mother's truth-demanding gaze. "I don't remember," she said. "I had so many dreams in the night, I can't tell what was dreams and what they did in real life."

I took the dolly from Matti, though he didn't want to let it go and he hunched right next to me to keep looking at it. "Unwrap it," he said. "See if it's alive."

But I couldn't; its little old face was too dignified. Some precious wood, it was carved of, gone dark over many years. And it was just about to say something terribly wise, I was sure. I didn't want to speak, in case I interrupted its thoughts, or talked over it and missed the words.

"Well, wife," said Father. "I haven't got time for this. If they're to go to old mother Chava, you will have to take them, for I must get to work. And Leah and Matti, I'll need both your helps today. Let's wash and eat quickly, and begin."

Yes, so it was one of those mornings—no play, just cutting leather into the smooth curved shapes that would protect people's irregular feet, and punching the hundreds of holes around the edge for my father's stitching to go through. He was in a very good temper because of the extra custom the holiday had brought; he hummed as he worked, and returned any greetings that were thrown in the door from the street, though he did not stop his work to make conversation.

"I am only taking the one of these children," Mother said at the house door. "I don't want to draw attention." She had the enormous child in her arms—was he even bigger now?—and little Shoshie was pressed into the doorway next to her thigh. "And I will bring this one back before I go to market; I can't carry him *and* the shopping."

She seemed full of doubt, but Father only said, "Go, go. If the others cry, they cry. It won't kill us."

"They're both clean; I checked. They're very—I don't really—" Matti and I looked up at her. Would she say it, would she be able to, the thing that would break the babies' hold on us? I almost felt she could.

Father fussily cut the thong he was working with, slapped down the sandal-sole and picked up another. "What?" he said, setting to work on it. "What's troubling you—that they're not *pretty* babies?"

She glared at him across the workshop but Father didn't look up. "I'll go," she said, and stepped out of the doorway, and wrenched Shoshie after her.

We worked on a while, and then Father said, "Thirsty work. Fetch us all a cup, Leah." Usually he sent Matti, who was more restless, on such chores, but today he wanted me, the eldest, to face whatever was out there.

The two remaining babies had unwrapped themselves, and they were busy on the floor, constructing something out of twigs from our kindling box, out of fluff that, from the color, must have been teased out of threads from our sleeping-blankets. They'd made little robes, little headgears, of their wrappings. They glanced up, their hands still busy. I did not alarm or interest them, and they went back to their work. I crossed to the water jar. Did they mutter behind me as I poured? I couldn't quite tell through the chuckle of water into the cup.

"Would you like some water too?" I said clearly, and I

poured them a cup too, and put it down beside them. They regarded the cup, and me, as if they'd never seen or smelt anything like us before, as if they were wondering what was good manners here—should they drink that stuff, or knock it out onto the floor, or pour it over their own heads, or what?

I whispered all this to Father and Matti as I brought in the water, watched them drink it and sat to my work again.

"Are they destroying anything, besides an edge of blanket?" said Father.

"Not that I can see."

"Well, we'll leave them to it. All this trade, we'll buy a dozen new blankets if we want."

Mother and Shoshie came home in a great ruckus not long after. "Look!" Mother cried at the entrance. "It's happened to them all! Yes, you go to your brother and sister, you little horror. Oh, what a business!"

"What are they making?" said Shoshie.

"I don't care. I'm just glad to have that squirming nuisance off me. He was *strong*! Look at this bruise!"

"Ooh, it's animals—look!"

"I don't *want* to look—"

There was a slap. "Ow! I only wanted to *see!*" Shoshie cried out. "I only wanted to *admire*—" Her voice went teary.

"Come away from them, Shoshana. They're nothing but trouble."

Then Mother was in the workshop doorway, Shoshie at her side as before, but blinking back tears this time, and her mouth pulled down. "Old mother Chava doesn't know *what* they are," Mother said to Father, "but she doesn't like them at all. She says we should have nothing to do with them. She says they'll eat us in our sleep."

"Hmph. Well, they had their chance last night," he said to the sandal in his hands, "and here we all still are."

"That's what I said. Star-children, I suggested, but she didn't know what that meant. She'd never heard of such a thing. That's neat stitching, Leah."

"She can do the plainer work quite well now, eh?," said Father. "Well, as long as they're not breaking anything, and not eating us out of house and home. For the moment, wife, I haven't the time to put them out on the street. I'll see how I feel when the holiday is over. They may not be pretty, but it's not as if they're in the way."

"Not in *your* way, maybe."

"Well, you throw them out, if they're in yours. Just choose a time when there are not too many people around to see. Or tie them up in a sack and carry them back to the dump, why don't you, and leave them there?"

"Carry them? If you'd see the trouble that one gave us—" She looked over her shoulder. "What's he doing, little naked —oh, he's making himself some clothes, like them. Husband, you should see this, he's so nimble-fingered." She wasn't going to suggest he put them to filling the sandal orders, was she?

"We're working here, woman. Don't distract my assistants. I've had to *turn away custom* this morning, can you imagine?"

She clicked her tongue and went away. "He was really bad," Shoshana said to Matti and me, wiping away the last of her tears. There was a red mark on her cheek where the little hand had struck her. "He wriggled and wriggled, up at old mother Chava's. He wriggled half out of his *clothes.* Old mother Chava and her daughter hated him, you could tell."

"Go and help your mother," said Father, and he fixed Shoshie with a look so that she would. "Have you finished that sole, Leah?"

I snapped my mouth closed. "Very nearly, Father, very nearly." And I bent to the stitching again.

Yoseph

I squat in the morning sun outside the stables, my new son asleep in my arms.

It was an easy birth. I'm glad of that; one can never be sure. I've seen some big women broken by birthing; I've been pushed from the room after one died, her baby still in her after a night and a day and another night of trying everything Mum knew to try.

"Forget this," Mariam said just before dawn. "I can't be bothered. Why did this baby have to choose *this* night, when we're bedded down in straw, among pissing donkeys and shitting cows? I'm just so *angry* at him."

I laughed. "It's good that you're angry. That means you'll want to push soon, and soon you'll push this baby out."

She sighed. "I just don't believe you any more. I don't think there's a baby at all. There's just a growth, and now it's too big to be borne and is killing me with these pains."

"This is all excellent news. I've often heard—"

"Will you be *quiet*?" She reared up in the straw, eyes glittering. "With your encouragement? With your unbearable smugness? So you've seen a thousand births? Well, I'd like to put you *through* one, and see how smug you'd be, I really would."

I nodded, ordering myself not to smile. "It's true, I am the lucky one in this stable, me and the donkey."

The night carried us on a little way past her outburst. Finally she stirred. "Where have the pains gone?" she said softly, curiously, all her anger vanished. "Is it over? Is my baby dead inside me?"

"The pains will come, don't worry." I drew in a big draught of the stable smells, and city smells from outside, animal dung and cooking fires. I'll never forget us there, the beasts' sleeping breaths heavy in the air around us, the dark ball of a woman in front of me, the night changing us from a couple into a family.

Then there was that sharp noise within Mariam, and she let out a cry, not of pain as I'd been hearing up to now, but of surprise and realization, as her waters gushed out into the straw.

"And very soon after, you came out squealing." I hold up little Emmanuel. His face pulls together thoughtfully, digestively, then releases into serenity. The skin of him is a wonder; the light of his very first morning glows in his cheeks, glows even brighter in his nostrils, shines *through*, almost, his tiny pointed fingers as they spread, purposeless, at his chin. What a thing, what a thing, an earthly boy, come into life.

Yes, earthly. I cannot yet see in him what Mariam's angel said, what my *own* angel said would be there. He's wondrous, yes, but only more wondrous than other babies because he's ours to keep close and care for; in other respects he's only flesh like them, only some tiny breaths and a few experimental cries. There is not a glimmer of the divine about him, no potency, no portent.

Should I be disappointed? I think of the angel that came to me, the size of it, how it streamed with glory, how its voice shook in my spine, in my bowels, uttering truths I couldn't question. I suppose I was expecting that sort of thing of this slip of a boy, expecting perhaps more than that, if the angel was only the messenger of the Lord, and this the Lord Himself.

But I look at him, and I touch his soft face, and it's not dismay that haunts me, but something like relief, something like hope. Might an angel speak so, and yet we be passed over? Might Mary and I have created those angels, out of our own fears and wants? Mad people believe entirely in their visions; might we not find ourselves to have been only a little mad, and to have fallen back to sanity, now that we have our perfectly unexceptional man-child safely delivered into our arms?

Leah

"Run and play," Father finally said, mid-afternoon, though he and Mother kept on working, when on a quieter day they might have slept the afternoon away.

Napping seemed to be the star-children's habit, too. "Look at them," said Matti as we came out of the work-room, "How polite of them, to line up there just the way we put them."

"See the little sheeps they made?" Shoshie went forward to pick one up, but the closest stiff-sleeping figure let out a low hiss and she leaped back to us. "They don't like you touching."

"Well, *that's* obvious," said Matti.

"Have they talked to you today," I said to Shoshie, "or have they just slapped you and hissed at you?"

She rubbed her cheek. "Sometimes I *thought* they were talking, to each other. But when I listened properly, I couldn't hear anything."

We ran and played, as Father had told us to. We actually did run, a lot, all around town; it was exciting, so crowded for the holiday. We could go anywhere; the usual borders between our territory and other children's didn't hold, not with so many extra families crowding in, not to mention donkeys, and cattle and sheep brought in for sacrifices and feasts. We went all the way across to the far side of the marketplace, into some of the lanes there, but then we got frightened of how far we'd come, and we ran home and sat on our step planning a second adventure, maybe as far as Rachel's Tomb.

We had just told a passing traveler how to find his way back to the market when I felt a hand on my shoulder. It was the star-girl, close behind me. I jumped up, and Matti and Shoshana were out of the doorway quick smart too.

The three star-children stood there, sober as census-men. Each bore a sheep that somehow, in spite of being made of twigs, managed to slump, to look heavy—and woolly too, thickly so, though they had taken only a few threads from that blanket of ours.

They stepped out into the street and passed us, the tops of their heads about as high as the middle of my thigh. One of the boys had the doll strapped to his back; it looked as if it were solemnly praying over everything behind them. They walked away from us with no word or wave of farewell.

"Let's follow them," said Matti.

"Let's not," said Shoshana and I together.

Matti raised his eyebrows. "Don't you want to find out where they're taking their little sheepies?"

"I'm just glad they've gone," I said.

"Me too," said Shoshana. "You should've seen old mother Chava's face. It was scary how scared she was."

The star-children walked confidently up the street, not like children at all—well, not like us. Grave, they were, not playful at all.

"Have they been here before, do you think?" I said to Matti. "And we've just not seen them?"

"It could be. See how nobody notices them? Crazy Hoopman there, he didn't even shout. You'd think little shrunkards like that carried sheep past his door every day. Maybe if they're not actually *calling* you from the garbage, or *living in your house*, you don't really notice them."

"And if they *are* living with you, you don't really see how different they are, how much they don't belong." I cocked my head to look after them, but that didn't help make their strangeness any clearer. *Just children,* sighed my common sense, blanketing the troubled part of my mind. *Nothing to be afraid of.*

Yoseph

I cock my head to look after the visitors—maybe they'll start to make sense before they disappear down the back lane. One of them feels me watching and reaches over to scratch his back. I shake myself and I walk out into the morning sun, turn around and search the sky above the stable roof.

"How could they see a *star*, at this time of day?" I say. "Maybe they looked in the night, while you were labouring, and marked the spot and came back when it was quieter."

There *is* something up there, but it's much more like a dimple than a star, much more like something in my eye than something in the sky.

Mary comes frowning out from the stable's shadows, and folds her arms over her still softly rounded belly. "I never thought of the danger, before."

"I didn't think they were *dangerous*, exactly. They just wanted to touch his . . . godliness, I suppose." Is his godliness something only others can see, maybe? Will he seem earthly to us forever, while other people see glory in him? Have we joined him in his godliness, so that we're aglow too, and can't discern any difference in him? I shake my head; there are too many possibilities. Yesterday things seemed so simple. Even last night, bringing the baby out, I wasn't being bothered by these doubts.

"Perhaps that wasn't very polite, Mariam, taking Emmanuel away like that."

"I know. But they smelt so bad."

"They smelt only of sheep. What can you expect of shepherds?"

"And then they wanted to touch him, and I had a sudden fear. It seems silly now that I talk about it, but I thought they meant to steal him, they reached for him so eagerly."

"It was peculiar, wasn't it?" I stand shoulder to shoulder beside her, and we both squint out into the glare.

"And even if they didn't take him, there was . . . Well, the touching. We will have to have some rules, Yoseph. Othewise, just think, anyone who wants to be healed will be pawing the boy. People with all sorts of illness—lepers, even."

"Will it matter, if he's the Savior and the Lord of All? Won't his holiness protect him?"

"I don't know. Do you want to take the risk that it won't?"

I think about it for a while and sigh. I wish an angel would visit us now. I wouldn't be struck dumb this time; I might have the courage to ask him some practical questions.

"Once the word gets out," Mariam goes on, "everyone will want a piece of this child. Think about it, Yoseph, the things he'll be able to do—the things people will *want* him to do. Anything the Lord can do, he can. Not just heal the sick but make food, make money out of nothing, knock down walls, explode mountains, change the weather, bring up game for hunters. Many people, I should think, would want to use him for their own ends. We'll have to be vigilant. Think of it! The politics! The armies he could raise!"

"Yes," I say, to stop her talking. "It's terrifying." I don't want to think that far, that big.

She leaves a pause, and then, "So I think we should have a rule. They can look at him all they like. They can look, they can worship, they can lay down gifts at his feet, make little sacrifices, but they *may not touch him*, with so much as a fingertip. Anyone who's not family. Any strangers. All right? If this is going to keep happening, people coming to worship, we don't want him being handled by all and sundry."

I think of the shepherd, the one who stood up first, how disgusted he looked when Mariam snatched Emmanuel out of reach, how he became almost rude. *Well, we've seen him,* he said to his fellows. *We've seen that it's true, what that angel said. We must go now, and . . . and tell everybody what we've seen, so that they . . . so that they know that the Savior has arrived, and come themselves to offer praise and thanks—and suitable gifts, those who can afford them.* It was as if he was making it up as he went along, reaching into the stable shadows after Mariam, and trying to sense what words might put him in her good graces.

And the others rose from kneeling too, and they looked all confused and disappointed too, the one with the sick sheep in his arms, the other with the lamb on a string. *I'm sure it's going to be an interesting journey, being parents to such a wonder,* said one of them. *So I wish you strength, you know, and steadiness. And faith, lots of faith.* They said all the right things but the tone they used was wrong. It was as if someone had told them how to be polite but they didn't feel it, just put out the words they'd learned and thought that would be enough.

Mary looks up at me when I don't answer her. I nod slowly. "I feel as if a storm is about to break on our heads."

She grasps my elbow. "We'll do right by this boy, and right by the Lord as well."

I search her face. How lonely we'll be, our little family, with the worshippers all around reaching for our child, calling for him, wanting a piece of him.

Did you see, I want to say, *as they left?* But I won't say it; I don't want to frighten us any further. *Did you see how the middle one, when he scratched his back, how the shadow of his hand on his robe was just like a monkey clinging there, looking back at us, grinning?*

Leah

Father had put us all back to work while the light was good. Even Shoshana was helping, rubbing oil into some sole-pieces with Mother looking on. And Matti was working without complaint for a change; now that those star-children were gone, perhaps like me he felt grateful for ordinary things, for right-shaped faces, for talk we could understand, for chores that made sense.

The afternoon was getting on when a hissing and muttering out in the lane made us lift our heads. "It's them," said Shoshie. "They're coming back."

I wouldn't want to have walked into the glare Mother sent out the doorway. But the star-children, their sheep toys under their arms, strode straight into the workshop—and started *rummaging*. "Hey!" said Father as one of them picked up his glue-pot and carried it off.

The boy with the doll on his back climbed to the money-shelf, opened the box there and freed a coin from the bag inside. "What do you think you're doing?" Father was on his feet, which made him just the right height for the star-child to jump onto his shoulders and, when his knees buckled, from there into the pile of leather scraps.

By the time Father swiped after him, they'd all moved on, in through the house door. Shoshie made to get up, but Mother held her back, so Matti and I both sat tight too, only Father going after them. Vessels clanged and sticks cracked, and there was a lot of sharp, spitty talk, and leathery feet slapping the floor, and robes flapping.

Father came back with the glue pot. "They took two little scoops," he said, "and put them in pans and tossed this away as if I wasn't right there needing it, for my honest work that put a roof over their heads last night." He sat back in his place and picked up the pieces he'd been about to glue.

"But what are they doing?" said Mother softly.

"Quarrelling. And building up the fire. It looks to me as if they're getting ready to cook up that coin and that glue. Into what, I don't know, but I'm not going to stop them. By the look, they'd bite me if I tried. And I've got work to do."

So we kept on with our work too, all ears as we stitched and cut and oiled. The star-children's talk died down to little outbursts now and then, but whatever they were doing kept them busy and moving, stirring, slapping back and forth, clapping pans on the floor or crunching them back into the coals. The heat came through the doorway almost as a wind. "They must be using up *all* our wood," said Mother. "You children will have to run up to market and buy more before dark—"

A flash of white light interrupted her. Our hands stilled, and then Matti could stand it no longer; he put aside leather and knife and leaped for the house door.

"Matti, no!" Mother was up and after him, but then whatever she saw beyond him transfixed her, and she stood there with her hand on his shoulder. And so the rest of us, even Father, followed, and before long we were not just at the doorway but in the house itself, spilled along the wall and watching.

Nimble-fingered, Mother had called them, but such deftness, in people so small, chilled me. They still seemed very angry, and this made them work even faster than we'd all been working in the sandal shop, springing from one task to another. They had dug in among our kitchen stores—the grain sack lay tipped and spilling, and Mother's herb pouches were sampled and scattered all over the floor—and the doll and the three toy sheep lay among them. The salve-pot was on its side there, too, every last smudge scoured out. From these and our coin and glue, and from who knows what other substances they had brought home on their persons, they were creating three marvelous concoctions. One pot brimmed gold on the fire, and every time they made a move near it a white flash happened like the one that had drawn us here. The star-girl thoughtfully stirred, in the second pot, what looked like several stones in some fizzing pale brown liquid, which filled the room with a swooning, spicy smell. This was cut through with something more bitter from the third pot, in which one of the boys had worked up the other portion of the stolen glue into half a potful of shining paste, which he was turning and turning with a spoon.

"What is this all *for?*" Mother wondered, but nobody answered her; we were all too busy watching, and trying to take into our nostrils as much of the rich scents as we could breathe. The star-children were so odd; they were so tiny, yet they had such smooth, practiced ways of moving, such cold, clever faces! Between scaring ourselves with the sight of them, admiring the beauty of the gold's turmoiling surface and dreaming of the worlds the scents spoke of—the high temple on one breath and the tomb on the next—there was no room left in our minds to wonder about human reasons, about likely, straightforward purposes.

It was a long preparation and a complicated one; the daylight had almost gone when they finished. They laid out all that they had conjured in the light of the dying fire: a pile of coins and three tiny crowns, all fashioned of purest gold though the coin they had begun with was only silver; nuggets of more translucent gold, which Father recognized as the resin the priests burn in ceremonies and processions; and redder chunks that had eventually solidified out of the shining paste. "That looks like myrrh," murmured Mother, "that you put in salves and anointments, if you have the money for it. But that comes from a tree, like the frankincense—you don't boil it up like that."

They took—from their garments or the air, I didn't see—a bag for the coins and two boxes, of two different woods, for the two resins. The girl picked up the toy sheep, and with some deft tweaking of necks and legs and fleece she transformed each one into a toy camel. The doll she unwrapped; I watched as closely as I could, and that tiniest person's leg did seem to move under her attentions, but I could not be sure; perhaps it was only a flicker of the firelight. She stroked the figure and hissed quietly over it, then wrapped it again with great care, murmuring all the while as if laying her words on it and securing them with the tapes.

The three of them came to a pause, each looking to the other two to confirm that everything necessary had been done. Then each picked up a crown, and placed it on his or her head. Matti and I clung tighter to Mother, and she to us, and over by Father Shoshie let out a cry of admiration—because when had we ever before seen people suddenly flushed with kingliness? It purpled and weighted and embroidered their garments, lengthened their hair and gave it a rippling shine, bejeweled their fingers and hid their feet in fine slippers, straightened their backs and narrowed their faces and gave a noble glint to their eyes. Only the doll stayed plain, stayed still. It gazed into the rafters as if none of these wonders was wondrous enough to waste its attention on, to be worth disturbing its tranquility for.

The kings exchanged some quick word noise, and one king tied the doll onto his back, and each picked up a frail camel-toy and one of the gifts in its bag or box. And then they had slipped out the door into the evening, and we remembered who we were, and that we had bodies of our own, bodies that would always be leather-workers' bodies and never kings', bodies that hadn't moved for a good long while, and that we must pull free from each other and separate from the wall, for the time of marvels was over. Our home seemed very still, very dull, very humble. Yet I felt relief, too, as if a storm had just passed on, having shaken things up, broken this or that, but not actually damaged any of us.

"And now the light's gone," said Mother, "and we've still all those sandals to make. And this mess to clean up too! Where to begin?"

Yoseph

I've just been to the well for a pot of water, to cook the fowl in that I bought us at the market. I'm still all warm and trans-formed from becoming a father; I've been keenly watching all ages of children along the way, and the way their parents reprimand or enjoy them. Having little Emmanuel out in the world has wrought a great change; before, he was only an idea installed in his mother, indivisible from her, a feature of her silhouette, an aspect of her personality. Now he's a separate being, and that's going to require different things of me.

I turn in at the stable yard. A little water slops over the pot's edge as I start at the sight of three great camels standing there with fine saddles and cloths and excellent harness. Two tower above me, while the third is folded to the ground beside them, and they all wear a disgusted look, as if it's beneath them to have to confine themselves in such a place. And this, what's this bothering them now? Oh, a *carpenter*? Must they really associate with one so lowly?

Mariam's voice reaches me, soft and flustered. "Gifts?" she says. "Well, certainly. I'll—I'll fetch him out, then, shall I?"

"If you would be so kind," says a smooth, foreign voice.

They're clustered in the shadow of the stable eave. A fall of purple cloth and an embroidered slipper is all I can see of them, and then that's gone as they follow Mariam in deeper.

By the time I edge around the camels and put down the pot and enter the stable, one of them has lifted my son from the manger and is holding him high as if offering him up for sacrifice. Emmanuel squirms in surprise and gives a choked cry. The fellow with the thing on his head—it's a crown! they all have crowns!—he delivers a blessing in a deep voice and an incomprehensible language. It's the kind of pronouncement that ought to echo mightily in some marble hall, but even in this cozy, cramped stable it lifts the hairs on my head, every one.

I wait behind them a little way, too intimidated by their finery, by their smell of wealth and mystery, and by the closing phrases of the blessing, to push past and lay claim to the boy.

The king lowers him, hands him out to the other two. "A fine lad, look you. A fine lad. He will grow up strong, coming from stalwart peasant stock such as yourself, madam." His grand voice cracks a little, and there's a glisten of tears in his eyes.

"We certainly hope for strength for him," says Mariam politely, no doubt thinking, as I am, *Peasant stock? Has he not eyes?*

The other two nobles hold and bend over Emmanuel. "Fine, indeed. Fine—"

"Oh, Yoseph, you're back," says Mariam.

No such faces have ever looked directly at me before—suddenly I see that I *am* a peasant, by comparison.

"This is my husband, Yoseph," she goes on. "Husband, these gentlemen have come to see Emmanuel. They saw the star, too, from—from their lands, a very long distance away, and they've followed it here to worship him."

"They have?" My voice is faint, but I'm lucky it's there at all. "That's nice." Incredible, but nice. I would like to think I'm not a shallow man, but it's true that while my wife and three greasy shepherds could not shake my doubts about the angels' words, the instant three well-dressed foreigners turn up I'm ready to believe in my son's divinity.

"You must be very proud." The nearest king hands me the baby with a smile. "That the Lord chose your wife as His vessel on earth."

I feel it, then, the Spirit in my spine, in my skull, humming at the touch of the baby. I wish I could see Emmanuel's face, which in the dimness is such a blur that he could be anybody's. "Of course," I say. "Very proud." And I back away from them to let more light in so we all can look at the child, but also so that I can be sure it's not just the presence of the kings that is thrilling me, that it's the little Lord in my arms.

"A handsome child, as of course he would be," says one of the closer kings.

"Why, thank you," I say, "although of course I can't take any credit for that."

Their faces are too foreign, too noble, too used to disguising themselves, out of politeness, or for politics, to show any reaction to my words. I look down at the baby so as not to stare rudely, and everything stops making sense. This is not my son. This is a different baby, quite different, just as this man's face before me is a different kind of face, a kind I can't read.

"You work in wood, your wife says?" The king's words don't carry any meaning, for a moment. *Work in wood—*

does he think I'm a timber trader? Why would Mariam have told them that? I have gaped at him, and mouthed *work in wood,* before the sense of it hits me. "Oh, I'm a carpenter, yes. Yes, I work in wood." The evening light shows me every unbelievable thing about the three of them: the blue and purple robes, the jewels swelling out of their finger-rings and crowns, the shining oiled hair. Perhaps it's some spicy perfume in that hair that is throwing my mind off, splitting things from their words, words from their meanings, enlarging the world and stuffing it full of dangerous, unfathomable powers.

I search out Mariam's face, nervous and a-glow, among them. I want to *be* her, at the back of these men, out of their sight and consideration. Not wanting to frighten her with my desperation, I glance down at the baby, and I can feel the awful moment passing; I can see Emmanuel's face coming back to me out of this stranger's. It was a mistake of my own mind, my tiredness, maybe; there's nothing wrong with the boy. It's just the thought of him being godly, Son of the Name, that made his face seem strange to me, just as before, when I was convinced he was mine, all sorts of his features and manners seemed to be reflections of my own.

"Please, be seated," says the king who did the blessing, as if this were his palace and he the gracious host. "We have gifts for His Holiness, and would like to present them." And he leads the other two out into the yard.

"Very well," says Mariam, and she eases herself down right there against the doorpost, then beckons to me for the baby. The kings go to their camels, and each digs about in a saddle-bag.

"Here he is." I lower the baby to her. Will she notice anything different about him? Will she baulk at taking him?

She gathers him in against her, and I relax. *I'm just tired. I'm just tired and surrounded by surprising strangers.* And I kneel beside her as she rearranges his wrappings, and we wait for the kings to bring their gifts.

Leah

It was good to have work for our hands. We were not to hurry, Father said, even if we had lost so much time watching the star-children. Hurrying would only lead to mistakes, which would mean re-working and no saving of time at all. If anything we should work a little slower, to make up for our tiredness and the distraction of our thoughts.

And they were very distracting. The warm soft gold being pulled and hammered into the crown-shape; the star-girl's long nose sniffing the dark paste; the boy's leap towards the kitchen shelves, to pick and poke among the possibilities there; the soft senseless voices blossoming and fading among the fire-crackles on the heavy-scented air—we had been privileged to see and hear all these glamorous and unusual things, though we sat here with the same old tools and materials, and the only smells in our nostrils now were leather and glue, Father's sweat, and the dust and dirt of our own feet crossed underneath us.

"We should have followed." Matti sank the knife-tip in next to the stiff sole template and began carving its curves into the leather below.

"We didn't have time," I said. "We had too much to do here."

"They would have invited us," said Mother, "if we were welcome to go with them. They would have let us know, somehow. The way they let *her* know they were from the stars."

She nodded at Shoshie, who was asleep under the shelves, the blanket with the frayed edge trailing out onto the floor from where she lay.

We worked, and thought, and occasionally spoke, and eventually I fell asleep over my stitching. Mother touched my arm. "Go out into the lane, Leah, and stretch and look at the stars," she said. "That will wake you up and keep you going a little longer."

And that was how I came to see the three kings riding home, on full-grown camels moving, gracious and slow, against the starlit sky at the head of our lane. Moonlight winked on the three crowns, and the three men towered above the houses in their gleaming robes.

"Mother! Father!" I called, but by the time they reached the door there were only three small children in king-costumes tripping along the lane toward us, with toy animals under their arms.

But no—one of them carried *two* camel-toys, and in another's arms lay a baby, a real, round-faced baby, in the kind of cloth everyone around here wraps babies in, and as wriggly as a real baby ought to be, its soft arms waving, its legs stretching and pulling up among the loose cloths, its starlit face creasing tightly, then opening up gummily, a little flake of a tongue there in the starlight, a little voice like a squashed lamb's bleat catching and creaking in its throat.

"The Lord help us," said Mother. "Whose is that, I wonder?"

Into our house the star-children trooped, and you could tell by their swinging walk and their proud silence that they had done what they set out to do, this time.

"No dolly!" whispered Matti to Mother.

"Well, no," she said. "They'll have swapped the dolly for this baby."

They took off their crowns and tossed them aside, and all their king-clothes and jewels faded back into their grubby white robes and brown skin, and their hair shortened and coarsened, and their faces lost their nobility and became weird and changeable again. Only the baby stayed the same, red and properly crying now, struggling in its wrappings in the star-boy's arms.

"What should we do?" whispered Mother to herself. "What *can* we do? What will they *let us* do—" And when Father appeared with a lamp at the workshop door, "Look," she said, "they've taken a . . . one of ours."

But now the star-boy strode up to her, and put out his hand, and when she laid hers in it he planted a gallant little kiss on the back before throwing it away with a laugh. Then he went on to Father, and the other two came to Mother, and the second boy kissed her hand just like the first, and the girl made a kind of bow, involving the skirts of her robe, and they both smiled up at her—though their smiles, in such faces, were not very reassuring.

Lastly they came to Matti and me, and the boys gave us quite hard slaps to the shoulder by way of farewell, and the girl kissed our cheeks and laughed, then pinched and twisted the places she had kissed, and laughed some more at our pain.

They turned back to each other, then. The boy stood in the middle clutching the screaming, struggling baby to his chest. He bowed his head and the other two joined hands around him, and the three of them began muttering. The muttering built to a yammering chant, and with a final shout they jumped, all three at once, and disappeared into a folding of the air.

The lamp went out, and we stood there in only the weak light from the work room.

Finally, "Ow," said Matti. "That girl pinches *really hard.*"

Father went back into the work room. We were about to follow him in and start work again when he reappeared carrying *our* baby, little Shoshie. "I think we should sleep," he said to Mother. "We can rise with the sun, eh? And make up some time then."

I caught up the frayed blanket edge as he passed. "See?" I showed it to Matti. "It really happened."

He danced away into the dark, danced back. "See?" he said, flashing a little crown at me. "It really happened."

Yoseph

Mariam kills the fowl and plucks it, and I fill our cook pot with water and set it over a fire of market-bought wood. We move about without speaking, pondering in our respective hearts what just happened. We settle ourselves outside the ring of hearthstones and gaze at the fire tickling the underside of our pot.

The first smell of the cooking chicken wakes me up, and I laugh. Mariam stares at me out of her silence. "Look at us," I say in a low voice. "Sitting over our pot outside a stable, when we could have king-food brought to us, in a room in the best inn in town. Have someone *thrown out* to make room for us."

She smiles and shakes her head.

"Will this go on, do you think?" I say. "Will people keep coming, and bringing us things?"

She turns to squint up at the stable roof. "As long as that thing's still there, I don't see why not."

The "star" is more visible as evening closes in, but still it's faint and fitful. "I can't imagine how they saw it from their far-distant lands, can you?"

"Or even those shepherds, from the nearby hills."

Emmanuel cries inside, in his manger cradle.

"Does he sound different to you?" I ask Mariam.

"Different?" she says. "Ill, do you mean?"

"More *knowing*," I say. "More *summoning*. Not as bewildered."

The fire lights up her patient smile. "I don't think they grow up *that* fast, Yoseph. Fetch him for me, would you?"

I go in and pick him up, and the motion silences him. I take him out into the wide evening and give him to Mariam, take the lid off the pot and give the chicken pieces an unnecessary poke. She slips him in under her garments and guides him onto the breast. "Oh, my!" She stiffens, her eyes wide. "He's *keen* this time!"

I sit close and peek in at the dark little animal latched onto her. "They've spooked me, those camel-riders," I say, as much to him as to her.

"Spooked you? Surely not."

"No, really. Hear how quietly I'm talking? I don't want anyone to hear us. I've never had such a secret to keep."

"Oh, but it's a wonderful secret, surely?"

"I don't know, Mariam. A sensible carpenter would never dream of this, of strangers strolling into his life, handing him a fortune and exacting no price for it."

"I suppose not." She gives a little laugh of disbelief. "It would be foolish to dream so."

"I know, and it sounds wonderful, just to talk about, just to dream. But when it happens, actually happens, when the riches are secreted away in the straw—" I'm all but whispering now. "All it does is fill you with doubt, with fear."

"Really?" Her face is a frown and a sympathetic smile combined. Under the cloth, Emmanuel feeds with little gulpy, satisfied sounds, almost like laughter.

"They have to have made a mistake, those kings," I say. "They *have* to. It's all too lucky. They'll come back when they realize, and ask for their gifts back. I'm wondering, should we flee and hide? Will they know who to ask, to find out where we live? Will they follow us home?"

She puts a hand on my arm. "And what if they do? What if they do take back their gifts? Are the gifts what this is all about? We will still have this boy, won't we, this marvelous boy, to whom all will flock because he is the greatest gift of all. Do you doubt *him*?"

She draws back the cloth, and there he is, much clearer in the firelight, his jaw working as he suckles.

I touch his little, holy arm, just to feel the grab at the back of my skull, the singing down my spine. She's right; who could claim, now, that this boy wasn't something special? You only have to look at him, to touch him and feel your bones respond.

"I'm afraid of him, just a little," I say.

"Oh, so am I." She rocks toward me, firelight dancing on her smiling cheek. "And so we should be, don't you think? For who knows what he will be, what he will do, this little miracle of ours?"

Leah

It was just as well that we slept, because when we woke next morning, the workshop was stacked with all the ordered sandals, better finished than we could ever have done them ourselves in our exhaustion and worry. Firewood was piled by the hearth, and the pots the children had ruined with their cooking had been replaced with shining new ones. A new blanket lay rolled and tied under the work-room shelves where Shoshie had fallen asleep.

"Have they put back the coin?" said Matti, looking up at the money-box on the highest shelf.

"I don't care," said Father. "Three golden crowns make for more money than that box has seen in all its life, or would ever have been likely to see."

"Which is all very nice for us," said Mother, standing there with the crowns up her arm like bangles, "but somebody has lost their baby, and has only that loathsome doll instead."

"*Was* it a doll?" said Matti. "I'm sure I saw its eyes open a couple of times."

"Ha," said Father, "if that doll has half the abilities of any one of those creatures last night, we are all in for an interesting time."

MARGO LANAGAN has published five collections of short stories (*White Time, Black Juice, Red Spikes, Yellowcake* and *Cracklescape*) and two dark fantasy novels, *Tender Morsels* and *The Brides of Rollrock Island* (published as *Sea Hearts* in Australia). She is a four-time World Fantasy Award winner, and her work has also won and been nominated for numerous other awards, most recently the Carnegie Medal, a British Fantasy Award and the International IMPAC Dublin Literary Award. Margo lives in Sydney, Australia.